DATE DUE

Bugs That Live On Animals

Kirsten Weir

Marshall Cavendish Benchmark
New York

Marshall Cavendish Benchmark
99 White Plains Road
Tarrytown, NY 10591
www.marshallcavendish.us

All Internet addresses were available and accurate when this book was sent to press.

Library of Congress Cataloging-in-Publication Data

Weir, Kirsten.
    Bugs that live on animals / by Kirsten Weir.
        p. cm. -- (Bug alert)
    Includes bibliographical references and index.
    ISBN 978-0-7614-3189-3
1. Parasites--Juvenile literature. I. Title.
    QL757.W37 2009
    595.717'857--dc22
    2008014824

The photographs in this book are used by permission and through the courtesy of:

Half Title : STEVE GSCHMEISSNER/SPL/Photolibrary
Jaroslaw Wojcik/ Istockphoto : P4 ; Derek Bromhall/ Oxford Scientific / Photolibrary : P5 ; Dennis Kunkel/ Phototake
Science/ Photolibrary : P7 ; David Scharf/ Gettyimages : P9 ; Troy Bartlett / Alamy : P11 ; Cath Wadforth/SPL /
Photolibrary : P13 ; CROWN COPYRIGHT COURTESY OF CSL/SPL /Photolibrary : P15 ; ANDREW SYRED / SPL/Photolibrary :
P17 ; Mircea BEZERGHEANU/ Shutterstock : P18 tr ; STEVE GSCHMEISSNER/SPL/Photolibrary : P19 ; CAROL GEAKE /
Animals Animals / Photolibrary : P21 ; RICK HALL/ CMSP Images : P23 ; Robert Shantz / Alamy : P25 ;
Heinz Krimmer / voller Ernst/ Photolibrary : P27 ; Andrey Novikov/ Dreamstime : P29.
Cover photo: David Burder/ Gettyimages
Illustrations : Q2A Media Art bank.
Illustrators: Indranil Ganguly, Rishi Bhardwaj, Kusum Kala, Pooja Shukla

Created by: Q2A Media
Creative Director: Simmi Sikka
Series Editor: Maura Christopher
Series Art Director: Sudakshina Basu
Series Designers: Mansi Mittal, Rati Mathur and Shruti Bahl
Series Illustrators: Indranil Ganguly, Rishi Bhardwaj, Kusum Kala and Pooja Shukla
Photo research by Anju Pathak
Series Project Managers: Ravneet Kaur and Shekhar Kapur
Printed in Malaysia

135642

Contents

The World of Bugs

What is a bug? People often use the word to mean insects. Insects are animals with six legs and bodies divided into three segments. Many people, however, use the word bug to describe other kinds of creeping, crawling creatures.

Most bugs are small. They live their lives without being seen by anyone. Still, bugs are more common than one might think. Out of every ten animals on the planet, nine are **invertebrates**!

Insects are the stars of the animal world. In terms of numbers, they are the most successful animals on the planet. As many as one thousand different types of insects can live in one family's backyard. Millions of individual insects may roam a single acre of land. Each year, scientists describe about ten thousand new kinds of insects.

Bugs by the Numbers

6: Number of legs that insects have

8: Number of legs that spiders, ticks, and mites have

0, 2, or 4: The number of wings that insects have

30 million: The estimated number of different kinds of insects on Earth

350 million: Number of years ago that insects first appeared on Earth

1/100 inches (0.25 millimeters): Length of the world's smallest insects

30 inches (760 mm): Wingspan of the largest insect ever, an ancient dragonfly found as a **fossil**

Wiggly Bugs

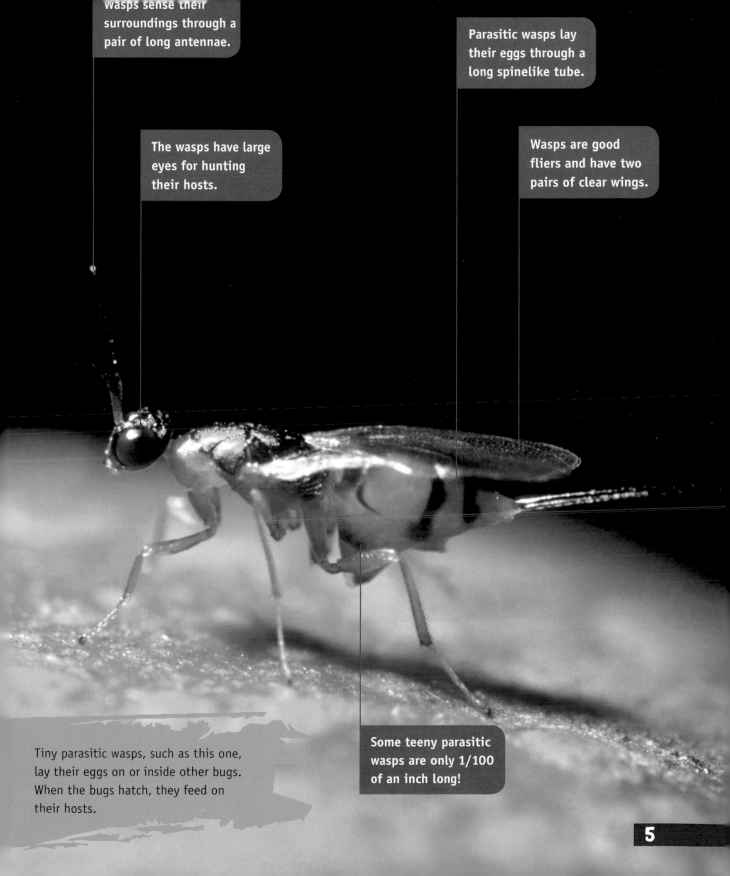

Wasps sense their surroundings through a pair of long antennae.

Parasitic wasps lay their eggs through a long spinelike tube.

The wasps have large eyes for hunting their hosts.

Wasps are good fliers and have two pairs of clear wings.

Tiny parasitic wasps, such as this one, lay their eggs on or inside other bugs. When the bugs hatch, they feed on their hosts.

Some teeny parasitic wasps are only 1/100 of an inch long!

5

Parasites

Bugs that live on or in other animals are called parasites. The animal that a parasite lives on is called its host. Hosts give parasites a place to live and food to eat. While a parasite benefits from the relationship, the animal host is harmed by it.

A Life on Other Animals

Some **parasitic** bugs live on other animals. Fleas, for instance, spend their days snug in the warm fur of cats and dogs. They provide fleas with food and a cozy place to live. In return, dogs and cats get itchy bites.

Other parasites are even creepier. Many of them live inside other animals.

A Dead Host

Another type of bug also lives on animals—dead animals. Maggots are the wormlike **larvae** of flies. (Larvae are the early form of an insect, just after it hatches from an egg.) They feed on the rotting tissue of dead animals.

Living Together

All animals, from tiny bugs to huge whales, have one thing in common: They all interact with other creatures. The area where an animal lives is called its **habitat**. Animals that share a habitat exist in groups called **communities**. Different creatures have different jobs within their community. Some animals eat plants, and others prey on animals. Some animals live on other animals. No matter what their lifestyle, they are all playing their part in the community.

Ant Habitat

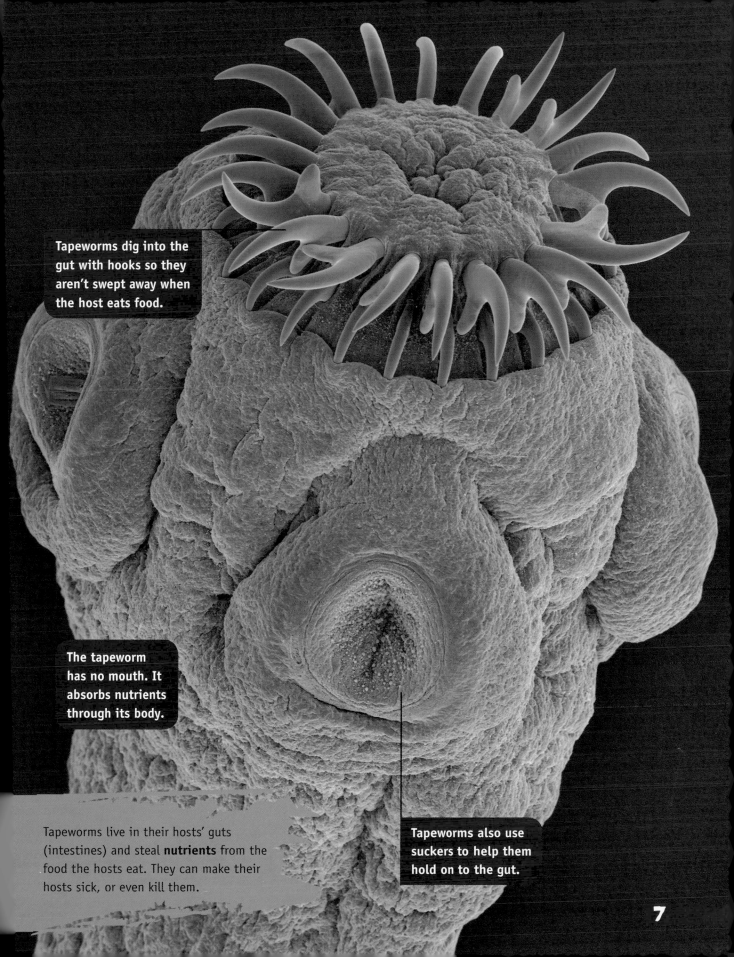

Tapeworms dig into the gut with hooks so they aren't swept away when the host eats food.

The tapeworm has no mouth. It absorbs nutrients through its body.

Tapeworms also use suckers to help them hold on to the gut.

Tapeworms live in their hosts' guts (intestines) and steal **nutrients** from the food the hosts eat. They can make their hosts sick, or even kill them.

Fleas

These tiny bugs can jump 7 inches (18 centimeters) high and 23 inches (33 cm) forward. On a human scale, those lengths compare to a person leaping across an entire football field!

What Are They?

An insect, the adult flea is only a few millimeters long. The flea is a parasite and feeds on the blood of animals. The flea uses its tube shaped mouthpart like a needle to pierce the skin of its hosts. Then it sucks up the hosts' blood.

Good Sense

While fleas have poor eyesight, they do have sensitive **antennae** that help them locate the body of a host animal. Fleas develop inside cocoon-like shells called **pupae**. Adult fleas will not emerge from their pupae unless they sense heat and vibrations from a possible host.

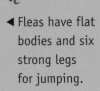

◄ Fleas have flat bodies and six strong legs for jumping.

Life Cycle

1. A female flea can lay as many as 500 eggs. Worm-like baby fleas called larvae hatch from the eggs.
2. Larvae feed on flea droppings, flakes of skin, and dried blood.
3. After a few weeks, larvae spin little cocoons called pupae, where they develop into adult fleas.
4. In about a week, adult fleas emerge and begin to feed.

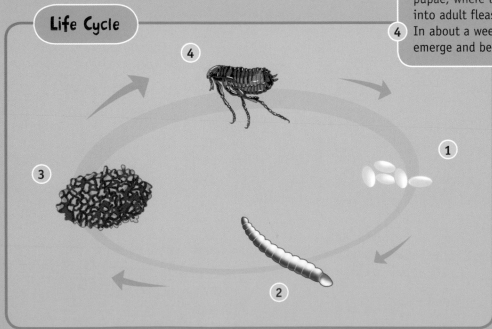

Life Cycle

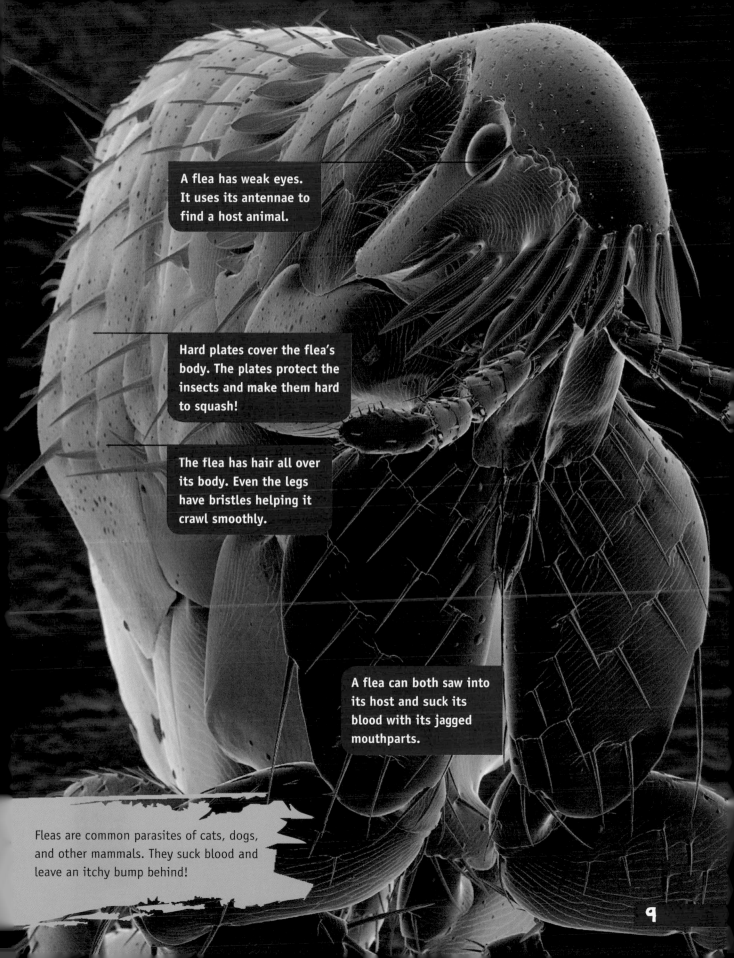

A flea has weak eyes. It uses its antennae to find a host animal.

Hard plates cover the flea's body. The plates protect the insects and make them hard to squash!

The flea has hair all over its body. Even the legs have bristles helping it crawl smoothly.

A flea can both saw into its host and suck its blood with its jagged mouthparts.

Fleas are common parasites of cats, dogs, and other mammals. They suck blood and leave an itchy bump behind!

Ticks

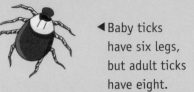

Ticks are tiny, blood-sucking machines. Different kinds of ticks live on different animal hosts, including cats, dogs, deer, mice, pigs, lizards, and people. Ticks often carry diseases and can infect their hosts with these diseases.

◄ Baby ticks have six legs, but adult ticks have eight.

What Are They?

Ticks are **arachnids**, eight-legged cousins of spiders. They suck their hosts' blood through needlelike mouthparts. These mouthparts are barbed like fishhooks. The barbs catch in their hosts' skin, making ticks hard to remove. Some ticks also have a sticky substance in their saliva, which glues ticks to their hosts.

Hard or Soft?

Two different types of ticks exist: hard ticks and soft ticks. A hard outer shell covers hard ticks. Soft ticks do not have a hard shell.

Life Cycle

1. A female tick lays thousands of eggs on plants or on the ground.
2. Young ticks, called larvae, hatch from the eggs.
3. The larvae look for an animal to feed on.
4. After eating, they drop to the ground and shed their skin. They are called **nymphs**.
5. The nymph looks for another host to feed on. After feeding, it will shed its skin and become an adult.

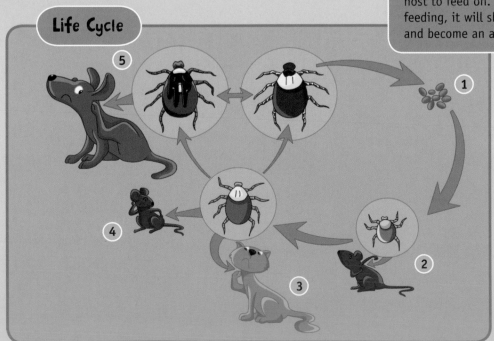

Life Cycle

Most ticks have poor eyesight.

Immature ticks can be smaller than the period at the end of this sentence.

A female tick can lay as many as 18,000 eggs before she dies.

Ticks have spiny legs with claws at the end. Ticks use the spines and claws to hang on to grass, branches, and other plants. When an animal host walks by, the tick hops on and starts to feed.

Ticks have special sense organs on their front legs that help them find animal hosts. The organs detect the breath, heat, and movement of nearby animals.

Many ticks carry diseases. The human illness called Lyme disease is spread to people by deer ticks. The American dog tick (pictured here) doesn't carry Lyme disease.

Ticks' bodies are made up of a tiny head and a round abdomen. The abdomen swells like a balloon as it fills with blood.

Mites

Mites are everywhere, from the freezing North Pole to the hottest desert. They live under the skin of turtles and inside the fur of family pets. Because mites are usually less than .04 inches (1 mm) long, they can hide right under our noses.

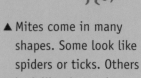

▲ Mites come in many shapes. Some look like spiders or ticks. Others look like tiny crabs.

What Are They?
Like ticks, mites are also arachnids. They have eight legs and are usually tiny. As parasites, mites feed on the blood of their hosts. Thousands of mite species exist. They can live on birds, mammals, reptiles, and even other bugs.

Itchy and Scratchy
Parasitic mites rely on their animal hosts to survive. These mites sometimes burrow into the skin of their hosts. They can irritate the animal's skin and cause a condition called mange. An animal with mange suffers from itchy skin and sometimes loses its hair.

Life Cycle
1. A female mite burrows into the skin of her host to lay her eggs.
2. Mite larvae hatch from the eggs.
3. The larvae make new burrows all over the host's skin.
4. After feeding on the host's blood, the larvae shed their skin and become nymphs. Then they shed their skin again.
5. As adults, mites lay more eggs. The mites will spend their whole lives on their host.

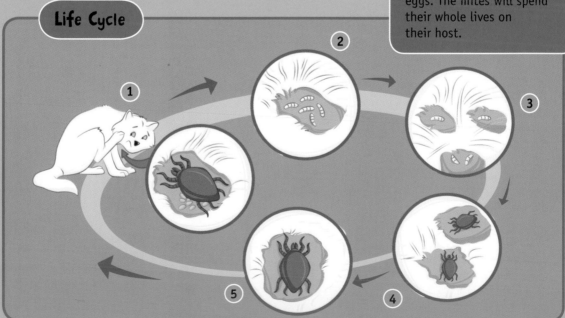

Life Cycle

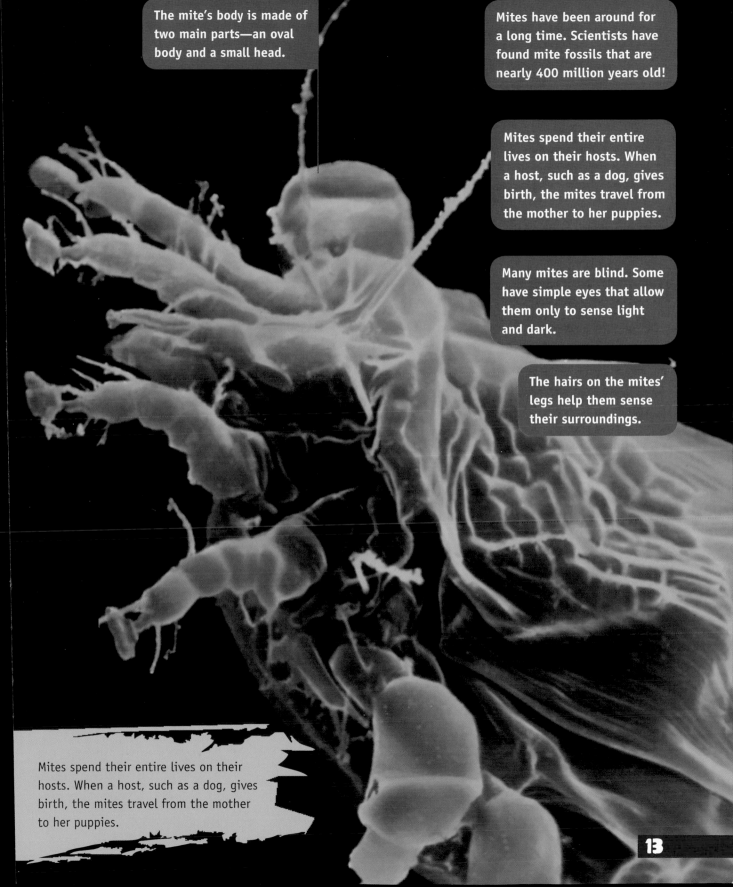

The mite's body is made of two main parts—an oval body and a small head.

Mites have been around for a long time. Scientists have found mite fossils that are nearly 400 million years old!

Mites spend their entire lives on their hosts. When a host, such as a dog, gives birth, the mites travel from the mother to her puppies.

Many mites are blind. Some have simple eyes that allow them only to sense light and dark.

The hairs on the mites' legs help them sense their surroundings.

Mites spend their entire lives on their hosts. When a host, such as a dog, gives birth, the mites travel from the mother to her puppies.

Bee Mites

Bees are small, but bee mites are even smaller. The mites are parasites on bees. The tiny parasites spell big trouble for the health of honeybees.

What Are They?

Bee mites, like spiders and ticks, are arachnids. They usually have oval bodies and eight legs. There are many different kinds of bee mites. Some live *on* the bees' bodies. Some live *inside* the bodies of bees.

Empty Hives

Honeybees **pollinate** crops such as nuts, fruits, and vegetables. Without help from bees, many of these crops cannot grow.

Mites feed on bees and make them sick. When bees are infected with mites, they have trouble fighting off other diseases. They can die from these illnesses.

Tiny Mites Cause Big Trouble

In the autumn of 2006, millions of honeybees disappeared from their hives. Some scientists think the bees were dying because they were infected with mites.

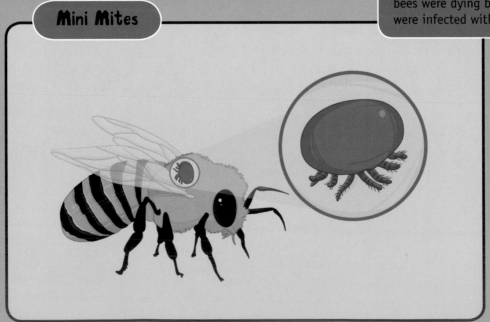

Mini Mites

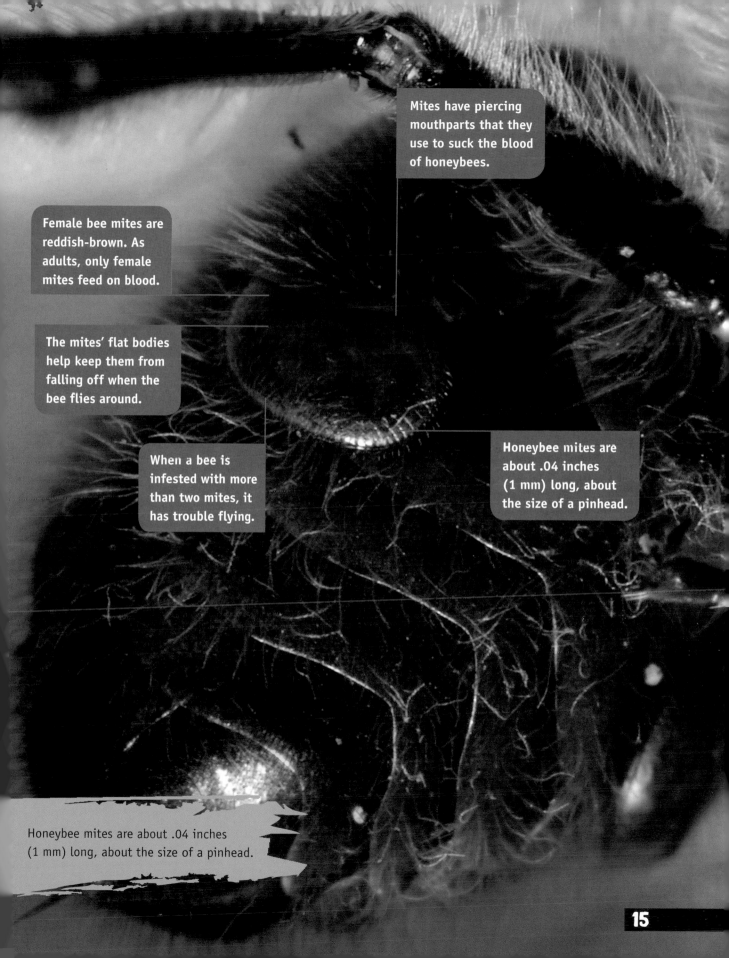

Mites have piercing mouthparts that they use to suck the blood of honeybees.

Female bee mites are reddish-brown. As adults, only female mites feed on blood.

The mites' flat bodies help keep them from falling off when the bee flies around.

When a bee is infested with more than two mites, it has trouble flying.

Honeybee mites are about .04 inches (1 mm) long, about the size of a pinhead.

Honeybee mites are about .04 inches (1 mm) long, about the size of a pinhead.

Fish Lice

You have probably heard of lice that live on human heads. Unlike human lice, fish lice can make their hosts sick—and even kill them.

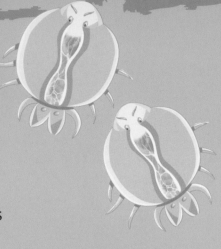

What Are They?
Fish lice look a bit like insects, but they are actually little **crustaceans**. Some fish lice can grow to 1/3 inches (1 cm) long. To a little fish, that is a pretty big bug!

▲ There are more than two hundred different kinds of fish lice.

All Aboard!
Fish lice feed on the blood and tissues of fish. As larvae, fish lice swim through the water or roll in a series of somersaults. When they come across a fish, they grab onto the fish's scales. When fish lice bite, they irritate the fish's skin. It may try to scratch its back against rocks or other objects to relieve the itch. If the bites become infected, the fish may get sick and die.

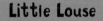

Little Louse

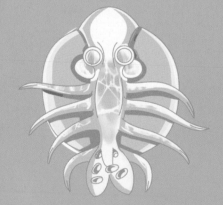

Not Really Lice

The lice that live on human heads are insects. Fish lice are not. They are actually tiny cousins of sea creatures like shrimps, lobsters, and crabs.

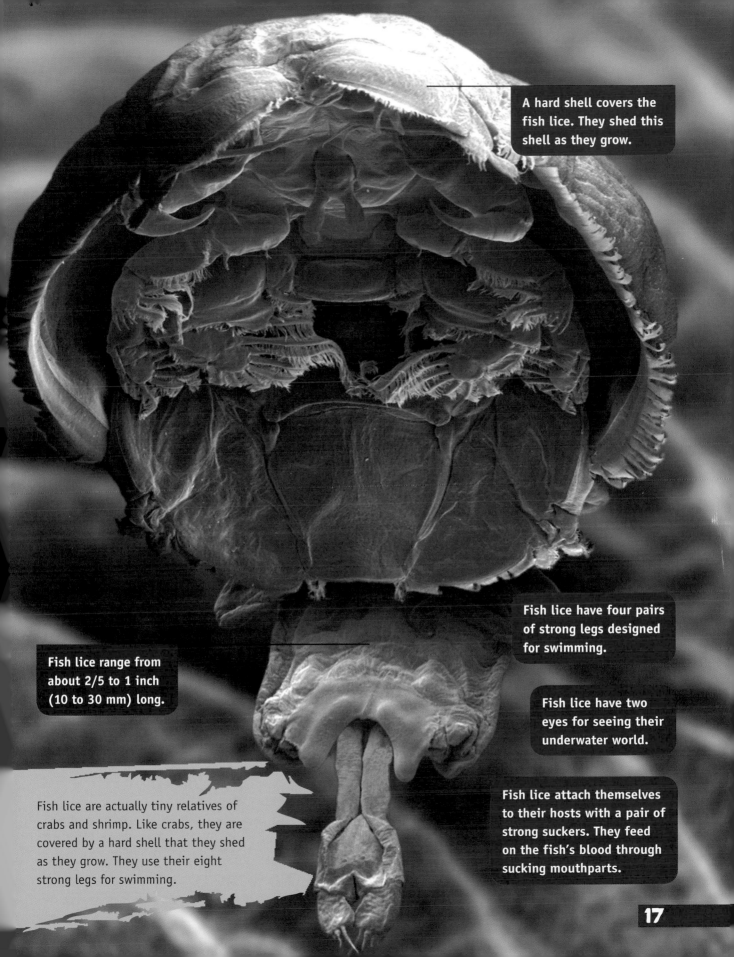

A hard shell covers the fish lice. They shed this shell as they grow.

Fish lice have four pairs of strong legs designed for swimming.

Fish lice range from about 2/5 to 1 inch (10 to 30 mm) long.

Fish lice have two eyes for seeing their underwater world.

Fish lice are actually tiny relatives of crabs and shrimp. Like crabs, they are covered by a hard shell that they shed as they grow. They use their eight strong legs for swimming.

Fish lice attach themselves to their hosts with a pair of strong suckers. They feed on the fish's blood through sucking mouthparts.

Leeches

Leeches can eat several times their own weight in blood during a single meal. They can live for more than six months on one meal!

What Are They?

Leeches are worms. Most live in ponds, rivers, and lakes. There, they suck the blood of fish and frogs, as well as of mammals such as deer that wade into the water. Other types of leeches live on land, mostly in tropical forests. Some land leeches prey on birds inside their nests.

▲ The leech's body is made of thirty-four segments.

Pain-Free Feeding

Leeches latch onto their victims with sharp, sucking jaws. When they bite, they inject a special substance that makes the skin numb. Leeches also inject a substance that thins the blood. The substance prevents a scab from forming, allowing the blood to keep flowing right into the leech's mouth.

Life Cycle

1. A leech lays a mass of eggs inside a cocoon that protects them.
2. After about two weeks, the eggs hatch. The baby leeches look like tiny versions of adult leeches.
3. The leeches make their way into a stream or lake. They feed by sucking the blood of other animals.
4. When the young leeches grow into adults, they lay eggs of their own.

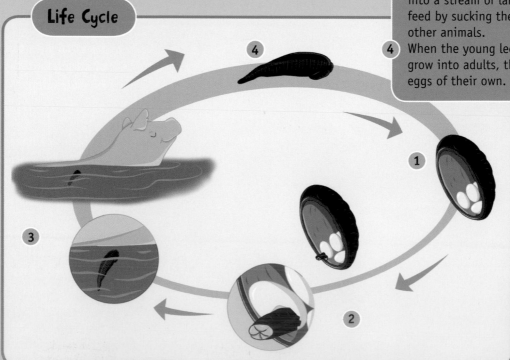

Life Cycle

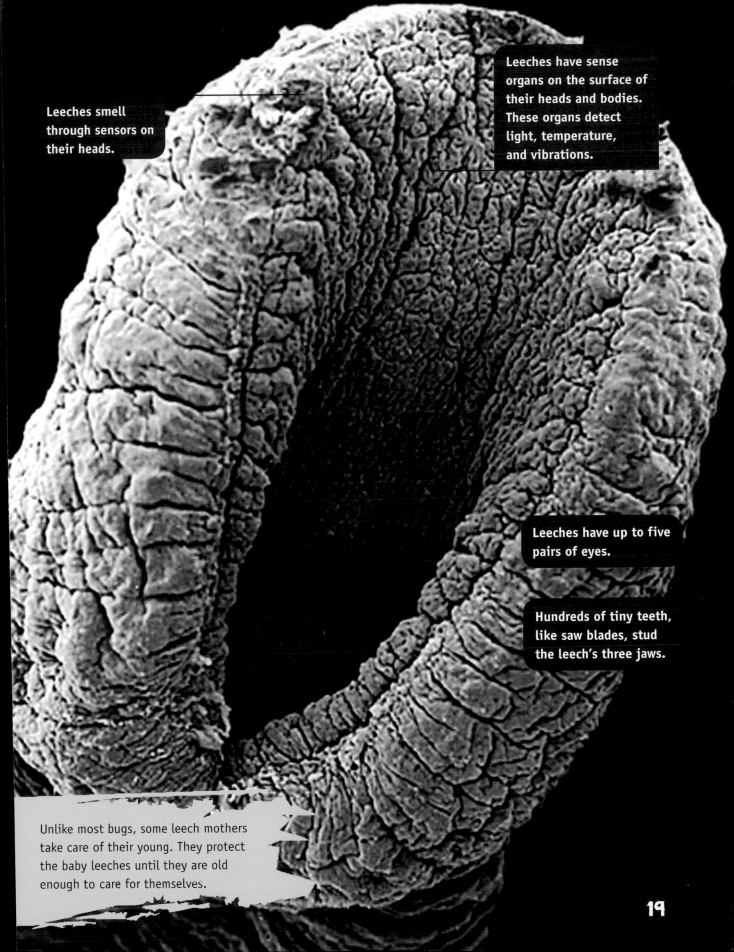

Leeches smell through sensors on their heads.

Leeches have sense organs on the surface of their heads and bodies. These organs detect light, temperature, and vibrations.

Leeches have up to five pairs of eyes.

Hundreds of tiny teeth, like saw blades, stud the leech's three jaws.

Unlike most bugs, some leech mothers take care of their young. They protect the baby leeches until they are old enough to care for themselves.

Bot Flies

Bot flies sound like the stars of a science fiction movie. The young flies develop inside lumps under the skin of animals. When they are fully grown, they burst out of the skin like alien life forms!

What Are They?

Adult bot flies are hairy flies that look a bit like bees. Their larvae are parasites. They attack livestock, such as horses, sheep, and cows.

Bellies and Noses

Some types of bot flies lay their eggs on the lips of horses. The horses lick their lips and swallow the eggs. The larvae develop inside the horse's stomach. Other bot flies climb into the nostrils of sheep. There, the larvae develop, safe and sound.

Life Cycle

1. Adult bot flies lay eggs on an animal, such as a cow.
2. Each larva causes a lump to form along the cow's back.
3. The fully grown larva breaks through the cow's skin.
4. The larva falls to the ground, where it forms a cocoon called a pupa.
5. After a short time, an adult bot fly emerges from the pupa and lays more eggs.

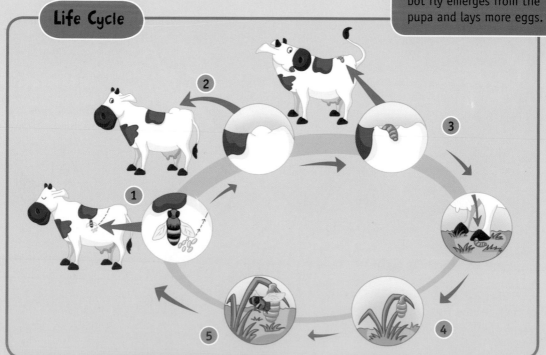

Life Cycle

Adult bot flies have six legs and two wings. They see the world through a pair of compound eyes.

Bot fly larvae have no wings, no legs, and no eyes.

Bot fly larvae breathe through small holes along their bodies. They make tiny holes in the cow's skin to get air.

Under the skin of the host, bot flies feed on liquids produced by the host's tissues.

Bot fly larvae look like worms. Adult bot flies have six legs and two wings.

Heartworms

More than one million kinds of worms live in the sea and the earth. The heartworm makes its home inside the hearts of dogs, cats, and other unlucky animals.

What Are They?

Heartworms are long, thin, threadlike worms. Adult worms can grow to 12 inches (30 cm) long. They are parasites on animals. The worms live inside the hearts and lungs of their hosts.

Heartfelt

Safe inside the body of their host, heartworms can give birth to thousands of larvae every day. These larvae develop into worms. Over time, the worms cause severe damage to the heart and lungs. If the infected animal is not treated, the heartworms can be deadly. Veterinarians can give pets medicine to prevent the worms from infecting an animal or to kill existing worms.

Life Cycle

1. Inside the host, adult heartworms give birth to larvae.
2. The larvae travel through the blood of the infected animal.
3. Mosquitoes bite the infected animal and pick up the heartworm larvae.
4. The mosquito bites another animal, passing on the heartworm larvae.
5. They travel to the blood vessels near the heart.
6. The heartworms become adults and give birth to more larvae. When a mosquito bites, it picks up the larvae and the cycle repeats.

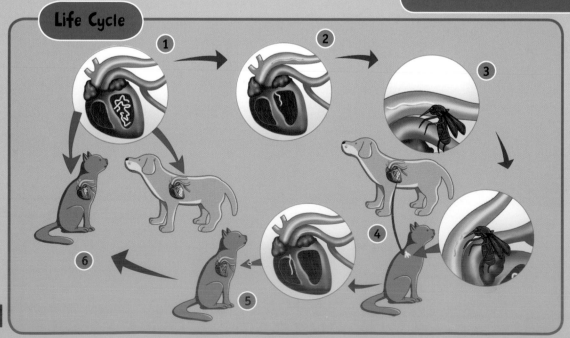

Life Cycle

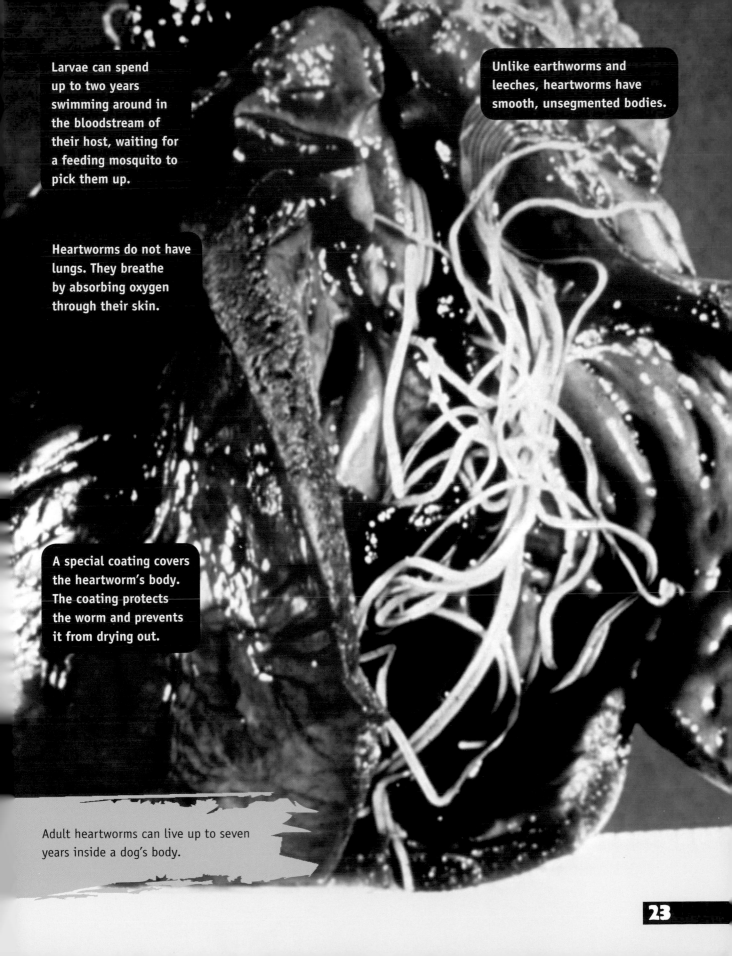

Larvae can spend up to two years swimming around in the bloodstream of their host, waiting for a feeding mosquito to pick them up.

Unlike earthworms and leeches, heartworms have smooth, unsegmented bodies.

Heartworms do not have lungs. They breathe by absorbing oxygen through their skin.

A special coating covers the heartworm's body. The coating protects the worm and prevents it from drying out.

Adult heartworms can live up to seven years inside a dog's body.

Tarantula Hawk Wasps

Even spooky spiders like tarantulas have enemies. Tarantula hawk wasps paralyze the spiders—and eat them alive.

▲
The sting of the tarantula hawk wasp is considered one of the most painful stings of any insect.

What Are They?

Tarantula hawk wasps are insects. They have six legs and two pairs of wings. Adult tarantula hawks feed on nectar from flowers. Their babies, though, are parasites.

An Official Winner

Two decades ago, students at an elementary school in Edgewood, New Mexico, discovered that their state didn't have an official state insect. They decided to hold a contest to choose one. Kids all over the state voted. And the winner was . . . the tarantula hawk wasp! In 1989, the New Mexico legislature agreed to adopt the wasp as the state insect.

Spooky Stinger

When an adult female is ready to lay eggs, she searches for a tarantula. She wrestles with the spider and stings it with her stinger. The poison sting paralyzes the spider. The wasp then drags the paralyzed spider into an underground burrow. She lays an egg on top of the spider. When the egg hatches, the baby wasp feeds on the tarantula.

Spider Sting

The tarantula hawk's stinger can be up to 1/4 inches (7 mm) long.

Tarantula hawk wasps are up to 2 inches (5 cm) long.

The tarantula hawk wasp has long legs with hooked claws at the end. With their legs, they drag paralyzed tarantulas into underground burrows.

Tarantula hawk wasps are found all over the world. In the United States, they are most common in the southwestern states.

Maggots

Wiggling, wormlike bugs, maggots feed on dead plants and animals. They break down rotting tissue and return valuable nutrients to the soil.

What Are They?

Maggots are the immature form, or larvae, of flies. The larvae are wingless, legless, and toothless. They can only eat liquids. Maggots spit a substance onto their food that makes it melt. Then the maggots suck up the liquid with their strawlike mouthparts.

Stinky Flower

Adult flies are attracted by the stink of rotting plants and animals. After all, they like to lay their eggs inside decaying matter. Some healthy flowers have found a way to trick the flies. The Asian plant rafflesia produces the world's largest flower. A bloom can measure 3 feet (.9 meters) across. The big flowers smell like rotting animals. The stench attracts flies, which pollinate the plants.

▶ When the weather is warm, fly eggs can hatch just eight hours after they are laid!

Life Cycle

1. An adult fly lays eggs on a dead animal.
2. The eggs hatch into larvae called maggots. The maggots feed on the rotting tissue.
3. After the maggots have reached their full size, they move to dry ground.
4. The larvae form cocoons called pupae. Inside the pupae, the maggots develop into adult flies.
5. After one or two weeks, adult flies emerge from the pupae. They will look for another dead animal to lay their eggs on.

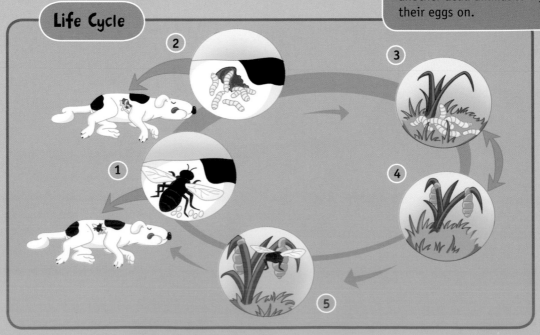

Life Cycle

Newly hatched larvae are 1/10 to 1/3 (3 to 9 mm) long.

Little, white, eyeless creatures, maggots look like grains of rice.

Maggots have no lungs. They breathe through tiny holes in their skin.

Maggots have no teeth and can only eat liquids. They suck up their food through strawlike mouthparts.

Stop Bugging Me!

For many bugs, living on other animals is a great way to survive. The animal hosts provide the bugs with food and shelter. Host animals, however, are bothered by the bugs. Fortunately, they have a number of ways to deal with pesky parasites.

While dogs and cats can have fleas, mites, ticks, and heartworms, most also have owners who can help them. Flea collars contain chemicals that kill fleas but do not harm the pets. Other medications can kill mange mites and ticks. People can also give their pets medicine to protect them from heartworms.

Some animals rely on help from other creatures. Ticks and bot flies can infest animals such as buffalo. These big animals let birds called oxpeckers eat the bugs. The partnership works perfectly: The birds get plenty of food, and the buffalo get the bugs off their backs.

Help for Humans

Chimpanzees groom one another, too, but they can do more to rid themselves of bugs. Chimps search the forest for certain plants to eat. These plants contain natural chemicals that kill some kinds of parasites that live inside the chimpanzees. Now scientists are hoping to borrow some of their medicine. Scientists are studying what kind of plants the chimps eat. They hope the research will help them find new medicines that can be used to cure people who suffer from parasites and other sicknesses.

Helping Hand

Monkeys pick bugs from the fur of their friends and family. They take turns grooming other monkeys in their group, ridding them of pests.

Bugs Data

Books

Davies, Nicola. What's Eating You? Parasites—The Inside Story. Cambridge, MA: Candlewick, 2007.

Hirschmann, Kris. Parasites! Lice. San Diego, CA: KidHaven Press, 2003.

Nichols, Catherine, ed. Animal Planet: The Most Extreme Bugs. San Francisco: Jossey-Bass, 2007.

Winner, Cherie. Everything Bug: What Kids Really Want to Know about Bugs. Minocqua, WI: NorthWord Press, 2004.

Internet Sites

Visit these Web sites for more information:

Insectarium: An All Bug Museum
http://www.insectarium.com/insectarium.htm

National Geographic: Parasites
http://www.nationalgeographic.com/parasites/splashframe.html

PestWorld for Kids
http://www.pestworldforkids.org

Glossary

antenna (plural: antennae): A feeler located on the head of insects and other bugs.

arachnid: An invertebrate with eight legs; spiders, ticks, and mites are examples of arachnids.

community: A collection of plants and animals that share the same environment.

crustacean: An invertebrate with a hard shell and jointed legs; shrimp, crabs, and fish lice are examples of crustaceans.

compound eye: An eye made up of many individual eye parts, each forming a part of an image.

fossil: The remains of an ancient plant or animal preserved in rock.

habitat: The area where an animal lives. host: An animal that provides food for a parasite.

insect: An invertebrate with six legs and three body segments; flies and bees are examples of insects.

invertebrate: An animal without a backbone; spiders, mites, and ticks are invertebrates.

larva (plural: larvae): The immature form of an insect.

nutrients: Chemical compounds that make up foods. The body uses nutrients to function and grow.

nymph: An immature tick, bigger than a larva but smaller than an adult.

organ: A part of the body that does a specific job, such as the heart, lungs, or stomach.

parasite: An animal that benefits by living off another host animal.

pollinate: To transfer pollen from flower to flower so that the plant can grow seeds and create new plants.

pupa (plural: pupae): A cocoonlike resting form of an insect; the insect changes from an immature form to an adult form inside the pupa.

warble: A bump on the skin of an animal caused by a bot-fly larva developing under the skin.

Index